I Can See

At the Farm

By Czeena Devera

I see a barn at the farm.

I see a chicken at the farm.

I see hay at the farm.

I see a cow at the farm.

I see an egg at the farm.

I see a duck at the farm.

I see a fence at the farm.

I see a goat at the farm.

I see a horse at the farm.

I see a pig at the farm.

I see a tractor at the farm.

I see a farmer at the farm.

Word List

farm
barn
chicken
hay
cow
egg
duck
fence
goat
horse
pig
tractor
farmer

83 Words

I see a barn at the farm.
I see a chicken at the farm.
I see hay at the farm.
I see a cow at the farm.
I see an egg at the farm.
I see a duck at the farm.
I see a fence at the farm.
I see a goat at the farm.
I see a horse at the farm.
I see a pig at the farm.
I see a tractor at the farm.
I see a farmer at the farm.

Published in the United States of America by Cherry Lake Publishing
Ann Arbor, Michigan
www.cherrylakepublishing.com

Photo Credits: © Bjorn Heller/Shutterstock.com, front cover, 1, 15; © Eric Isselee/Shutterstock.com, back cover, 5; © Peter Kim/Shutterstock.com, 2; © Tsekhmister/Shutterstock.com, 3, 11; © Anastasiia Malinich/Shutterstock.com, 4; © chattanongzen/Shutterstock.com, 6; © Stargazer/Shutterstock.com, 7; © Rena Schild/Shutterstock.com, 8; © M88/Shutterstock.com, 9; © Alexey Stiop/Shutterstock.com, 10; © ver0nicka/Shutterstock.com, 12; © ProductionPerig/Dreamstime.com, 13

Cherry Blossom Press is an imprint of Cherry Lake Publishing.

Library of Congress Cataloging-in-Publication Data

Names: Devera, Czeena, author.
Title: At the farm / Czeena Devera.
Description: Ann Arbor, MI : Cherry Lake Publishing, 2019. | Series: I can see | Includes bibliographical references and index. | Audience: Pre-school, excluding Kindergarten.
Identifiers: LCCN 2018034489| ISBN 9781534140356 (pdf) | ISBN 9781534139152 (pbk.) | ISBN 9781534141551 (hosted ebook)
Subjects: LCSH: Farms–Juvenile literature. | Farm animals–Juvenile literature. | Reading (Preschool)
Classification: LCC S519 .D479 2019 | DDC 630–dc23
LC record available at https://lccn.loc.gov/2018034489

Printed in the United States of America
Corporate Graphics

CHERRY BLOSSOM PRESS